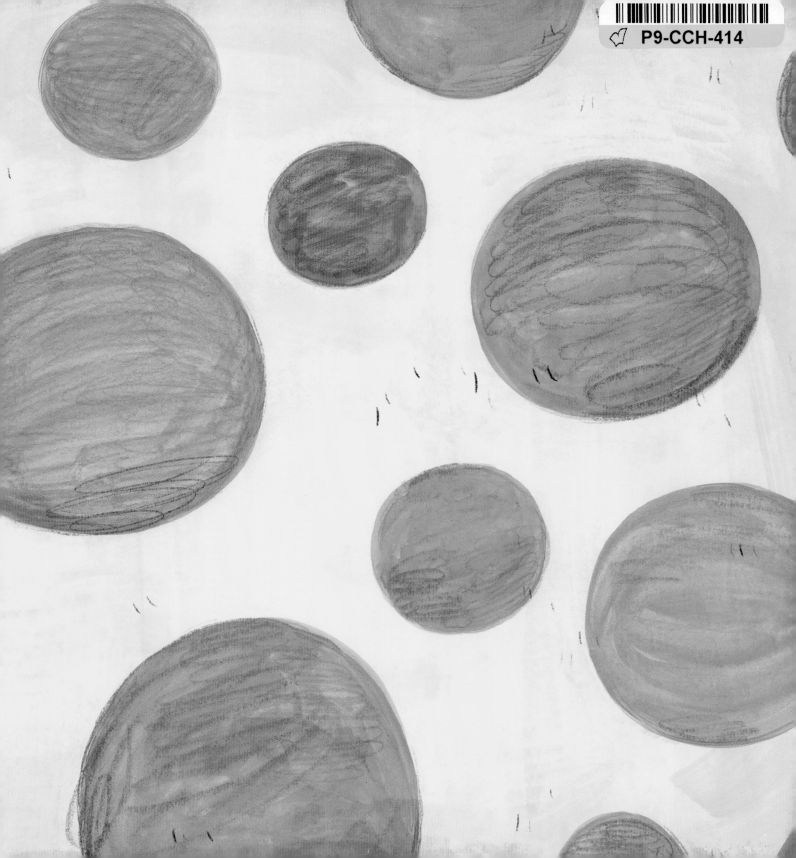

For my mom, who taught me to love books.
—LK

For Zelda, who inspires me to be brave.
—JS

Text © 2021 by Lisa Katzenberger
Illustrations © 2021 by Jaclyn Sinquett
Cover and internal design © 2021 by Sourcebooks

Watercolor, colored pencils, and digital painting were used to prepare the full color art.

Published by Sourcebooks eXplore, an imprint of Sourcebooks Kids
P.O. Box 4410, Naperville, Illinois 60567–4410
(630) 961-3900
sourcebookskids.com

Library of Congress Cataloging-in-Publication Data is on file with the publisher.

Source of Production: Phoenix Color, Hagerstown, Maryland, USA
Date of Production: January 2021
Run Number: 5021097

Printed and bound in the United States of America.
PHC 10 9 8 7 6 5 4

It Will Be OK

A story of empathy,
kindness, and friendship

WORDS BY
LISA KATZENBERGER

PICTURES BY
JACLYN SINQUETT

sourcebooks
eXplore

Every afternoon, Giraffe and Zebra
walked to the watering hole together.
But today, Giraffe couldn't go.
He would have to tell Zebra.

"Um, Zebra," Giraffe called to his friend.

Zebra twisted this way and that.
But he could not find Giraffe.

"Up here," Giraffe sighed.

Zebra looked up, up, up. Finally, he spotted Giraffe,
who was sitting in a tree, holding on for dear life.
"What are you doing?" Zebra asked.

"I saw a spider," Giraffe whispered.

"But you are bigger than the spider," said Zebra.

"Your eyelashes are longer than its legs."

"I am scared," Giraffe said, his voice soft.
"It might crawl up my hoof."

"But you are stronger than the spider," said Zebra.

"You're as solid as stone and he's as wispy as the wind."

"I am worried." Giraffe's voice shook like his knees. "It might chase me."

"But you are faster than the spider," said Zebra. "You'd leave him in the dust before he took a single stride. Come down from there."

Giraffe shook his head.

Zebra sighed. "It's just a tiny spider."

Giraffe understood Zebra's frustration. It did seem kind of silly being afraid of something so small. But no matter, he was scared.

He was worried.

He was embarrassed.

Giraffe expected Zebra to leave.

But Zebra waited.

And waited some more.

As the sun dipped down in the sky,
Giraffe searched for the spider.
He didn't see it anywhere.

Giraffe was nervous about getting down.
But his heart told him it was time.

So little by little, leg by leg, Giraffe
unwrapped himself from the tree.

"Thank you for staying by my side," Giraffe said.

"Even if it seemed silly."

"It's not silly if it bothered you.
I'm always here for you." Zebra smiled.
"Let's go to the watering hole."

Suddenly, Giraffe stopped.

There was the spider,
walking all alone.
Giraffe looked at the spider.

Then, he looked at Zebra.

With his friend beside him, Giraffe felt brave.

He bent his long neck down to the ground.

"Spider, would you like to join—"

But before Giraffe could finish his question,
the spider scampered right up the very same tree.

"He's scared of you now?" Zebra said.

"That's so silly!"

"Not at all," Giraffe said.

Then he stood by.

And waited.

Feeling WORRIED?

Do you ever feel scared, worried, or anxious? It's a feeling of big worry that can begin very suddenly (like if you see a spider). Or you can feel nervous or afraid about something that hasn't even happened (like worrying that you may see a spider). Most people feel anxious or afraid sometimes. When someone feels that way, it can help to share those worries with a friend. Talking about fears makes them seem less scary. It can take time for those anxious feelings to go away, and having a friend listen or just stay nearby can help. If those feelings are very big and overwhelming, talk to a caring adult for help. Can you think of a time when you felt anxious?

What can you do when you feel ANXIOUS?

Express your feelings—share your thoughts with a friend or trusted adult.
Take deep breaths.
Imagine a positive outcome.
Ask for help, or maybe just company.

Having EMPATHY

If you know someone is feeling scared or
anxious, you can help them by showing
empathy, like Zebra did. That means trying to
understand what another person is feeling.
In this story, Zebra isn't scared of the spider,
but he understands that Giraffe feels very scared.
That is an example of empathy. Can you think
of a time when you've shown empathy?

How can you help a WORRIED FRIEND?

Listen.

Stay with them until they feel better.

Don't try to solve their problem for them. Keep listening.

Share with them something that makes you scared.

If your friend is still struggling, it's OK to get a trusted
adult to help you.